The Beggar's Tomb
By Randall Hilt

To say that all reality is centered on a planet that revolves around a sun can be dizzying. But such is the case. In the material space that surrounds that world is an asteroid field. Some say it is left over bits from the mystery of creation. Some say it is the wreckage of the first war between good and evil. Only the Gods know for sure.

What people did know was that arcanium was valuable. And just like any valuable resource when it was discovered it brought the best and the worst out in people. Drake wranglers and rustlers, prospectors and outlaws, gamblers and pirates, these are the types that populated the Sky Planes. So, in a place known as the Town on the Edge of Night, in an asteroids field drifting through space, she plotted her revenge

One of the first things she had ever learned living on the streets was never gamble with a halfling. She was holding four dragons, and she had also quickly learned that males are fools when tempted with desire.

She shifted herself forward, showing off here equally exposed and ample cleavage. She was more endowed than most halfling women in this area, she knew. Another thing she had learned early in life was to never stand out. Now, she had to make her play, and she was going to use every tool she had!

She bit her lower lip and did her best to look confused and worried. Males liked to feel superior in every way, and she wanted this one to really feel confident. It also played to his desires more, drawing attention to her natural ruby red lips.

"I don't think I should bet this round," she stammered in a meek tone. " I hold," she stated and leaned back from her ploy of studying the game board.

In Dragon Toss you have to toss a card to bet. It can go to the discard or to the community card "Lair" section of the table. She had the best possible hand and was not about to let a card go to the discard pile, and didn't want to throw a Dragon into the Lair pile, yet.

Her opponent studied her, gave her a smile, and did exactly what she wanted.

"All in!" He said with a boast as he slid his chips into the pot. She could almost feel his arrogance in a tangible way. He leaned back and puffed out his chest, which still didn't pass his bulbous belly.

The male was a halfling who called himself Tex, a name he had gotten from his travels across the multiverse. He was a rich and powerful halfling male. So he was everything she expected; flamboyant, obnoxious, and indulgent. She had made him for her mark three years ago, after the tragedy, and the time had finally come.

She had never ran a mark so long. But she had never run a hustle this big, against one so protected. She spent the first year making sure he deserved this, it was hard to get evidence against the rich, especially when they own the law enforcement. Then she spent another year studying, his strengths, his weaknesses. She mastered his mannerisms, mingled with his henchmen and servants, and garnered their trust. The last year was putting all the pieces in play.

It all came down to this, she used lust to lower his defenses, and she would use pride to lower them further. *Males were such pompous fools.*

"Seems for such a well traveled gentleman, you have made a counting error." she smiled back, " I don't think my cards can beat yours, but I have more chips than you!"

Her statement made his eyes bulge a moment, just a moment, but brought snickers from the onlooking patrons. This worked in her favor too. *Weren't halflings supposed to be lucky?* She thought as she watched the final gear click behind Tex's eyes.

"Not so quick girly, if you're planning to raise me, you only automatically win if I can't cover yer raise with equal value! It doesn't have to be in chips!" He was boasting now as he tossed the deed to an asteroid mine on the table. He carried with him more often than not. He thought it worthless. He thought he was playing her. She had to make the next play perfect, time to really push his ego.

"I told you hours ago I was pretty good at Dragon Toss, but you probably weren't listening." She puffed out her breasts once more to emphasize her point, even licked her lips.

"I raise," she tossed a dragon into the Lair pile, " all in!"

The crowd had grown, and now audibly gasped as the card hit the felt. Throwing a Dragon on the Lair was often dangerous and usually a bluff, unless you had all four.

Corvaire, Tex's first lieutenant, shook his horned head. Light caught his ruby scales in a shimmering cascade. He was born of an ancient lineage of ruby dragons and men. He was male, but not a fool like his boss, he knew Tex was getting played.

"Now you have to figure out if you just got bluffed or beat by a pair of tits!" She pulled her shawl around her exposed self. The show was over. The play was over. She just prayed it was enough.

Tex barely took a moment to think, his face showed his frustrations with a bright red hue.

"Only a fool throws a Dragon in the Lair, I call!" Tex slid the deed into the pot and her heart melted. She almost lost control

The next few minutes were a blur to her. Tex turned over his hand, she doesn't remember what he had. It didn't matter. She couldn't lose the hand, the bet was the important part.

Tex threw some kind of tantrum,called her names, threatened her in all kinds of vile ways. He knew he got played. She wanted him to know.

The bouncers did their job and things quieted down. She collected her winnings, and herself, and left the gambling house. Her revenge was almost complete, now all she had to do was wait.

* * * * *

He waited in the shadows patiently outside the brothel.
Handsome and dashing with a perfect smile. He had spent
the last two years building his reputation as both deadly and
compassionate. It was all to win her heart, all to break her
heart. Disappearing for long periods of time, he had to appear
a mystery. *But it had to be done.* He thought as he stared
down the shadowy alleyway behind the brothel known as the
Honey Mine.

He soon heard her footsteps approaching and called out to
her with a low whistle. The halfling that owned the brothel was
a semi-retired pirate named Tex. A real bastard that abused
and controlled his male and female workers. Althea was
taking a great risk coming to see him. He didn't want to hurt

her. He had to emotionally, but he had sworn to do all he could to protect her from the physical.

Althea was beautiful, half elven with large almond shaped emerald eyes. Thin but fit, she was popular at the brothel. She, like so many, was addicted to the arcanium dust, a byproduct of the mines. She was one of Tex's most trusted whores. Not because Tex had earned her trust, like the handsome man had, but through fear and control.

"Did you bring the key?" He asked, pulling her into the shadows of his embrace. He kissed her before she could answer. If things were different, he could have loved her. He persevered then to do all he could to help her, when this was done.

She reached for his manhood, always eager to please. That's why he chose her. She had, a long time ago, lost her self worth. Now she sought it in the approval that came from pleasing others. And he had preyed on that pain.

"Not now my love," he said, pushing her away. "Our time will come soon."

Another lie, but justice has to be served, he thought. He kissed her softly, as lovingly as he could. *What could have been?*

The key in question was no ordinary key. Ordinary locks never gave the man trouble, having come from the dregs. This key held special enchantments to unlock the magical defenses of Tex's office and private quarters. Which, consequently, did give him problems.

The key also held magical defenses to protect itself, particularly one that made it impossible to pickpocket. Something else he was good at.

Something Tex was bad at, was keeping his ego in check. He was such a ruthless, abusive and miserable bastard that he never dreamed any of his servants would even dare to betray him. So he trusted his every need to his slaves, including locking up.

And so, he had come up with his plan. Have one of those servants steal the key as Tex was leaving; then he could enter the chamber and disarm the magical defenses while he was gone; then slip the key back into his pocket. Hopefully, all while he was, hopefully, distracted and humiliated.

The handsome stranger had considered using Tex's first lieutenant Corvaire . The dragon man lacked morals, obviously, but he was logical and grounded. A businessman, though unethical, the mysterious stranger had never seen Corvaire act even verbally abusive.

Corvaire was also loyal, something the scoundrel usually valued; but, it was not, unfortunately, something he had needed for this plan.

Althea was the best choice. The downward spiral of abuse, addiction, and eventual servitude had left her damaged, almost broken. And he had used the better part of the last year to rebuild her to fit his needs. Maybe he was no better than Tex, but justice had its price. And furthermore, he felt remorse. He didn't want her to be just another victim. He would find a way to do right by her, somehow.

He kissed Althea goodbye, whispered some insincere promise, and hurried off. He had to meet with a certain infernal blooded attorney before he made his way to the casino.

* * * * *

Tex was quite drunk when he stumbled into his quarters that night. Or, what passed as night in the Sky Planes, it was never really dark on any inhabited parts of the asteroid belt. The dark side was cold and needed strong magics just to venture through in brief stints.

Night here was just long shadows cast by the distant worlds of Arch'Onin and the enigma that was known as the Dark Stone.

It was during these long shadows that Tex had been humiliated. He had plenty of gold. The asteroid mine was just a bad old investment that he carried around with the hopes to pawn off on some fool. No, it was his pride that was taken from him. The halfling girly was supposed to be his conquest. Instead she defeated him publicly at a game in which he excelled. So he got drunk.

He got so drunk he never noticed the beggar that slipped his magical key back into his pocket. So drunk that he didn't notice the magical defenses the key deactivated weren't even up to begin with. So drunk he didn't notice the formless mass of goo under his bed. All as they had planned.

As Tex collapsed into the finest harpy down mattress gold could afford, the ooze began to lumber up from under where he lay. They crept over him like a warm blanket on a winter

slumber. This rest would last eternal.

They were slow and methodic. They had been patient this

long. They wanted him to sleep off some of the inebriation.

They wanted him aware of the justice he was about to serve.

They wanted him to remember and recognize what he had

done.

Nearly 2 hours went by, and the slimy form waited. Waited

until the guards had relaxed, maybe even dozed off. Waited

for Tex's stupor to subside. They had waited three long years

for justice, but this wait was the hardest.

But finally the wait was over. No sounds came from beyond

the abode. Tex had stopped slobbering and flatulating and

had slipped into a rhythmic snore some time ago. The guards had likely gone to sleep.

Tex was slow to wake and become aware of his predicament. At first, he had groggily tried to go back to sleep. Then he came to the realization he could not move. His eyes went wide with panic, probably thinking some sickness or magic had paralyzed him. Next the fright that he was restrained, not stricken. And finally, the color flushed from his face as he recognized the creature that was the formless plasma that engulfed all but his head.

"What is the meaning of this," he tried to bluster.

"Guards," he tried to yell, but his lungs had already been crushed enough to prevent any more than a strained whisper. They indulged Tex's last request anyway.

"Your sins are too great to count," the plasma creature whispered back, forming a head that looked like a gorgeous halfling with naturally ruby red lips.

"But the one that brought you to this end is by far the worst." They held there, forever perhaps, just to give him a chance to confess, to accept responsibility, to even acknowledge the gods be damned thing happened!

But he just stared back blankly at the face that had humiliated him. So they showed him. Every face of every beggar Tex had promised a chance. Every male, female, and child he had buried alive in his failed mine. Those thirty-six faces were burned into the ooze's memory.

His eyes got wider. He lost even more color. He began to sweat.

"That was an accident, that mine collapsed, there was noth..ugh.." The slime tightened their grip to end the lie. They wouldn't hear it! His breath was cut off. They felt a few ribs snap beneath their engulfing mass.

"I don't want to listen to the lies you told the public!" They hissed. "The sheriff confessed to the cover up when I killed him two years ago." His eyes were so wide with shock now, they seemed they would pop from his head. Or maybe that was from the constriction.

It had been a long three years. The first year after the incident the plasmic being had been spent investigating. They had their suspicions about Tex from the beginning. The sheriff had confirmed everything.

Time then seemed to stand still. They continued to squeeze slowly applying proverbial and literal pressure. They felt a few more ribs crack. Tex could no longer take the forces crushes his body. Eventually, his resolve did crack.

The ooze knew Tex would. They had spent two of the last three years studying him. They studied every mannerism. Every quirk was noted, every twitch was recorded.

"F..f..fine," Tex coughed and spit, both in defiance and defeat. A bit of blood stained his lips now. His face began to plum.

"They were worthless beggars, why do you even care?" He managed to ask through gritted teeth. She didn't answer, just continued her slow, deadly squeeze.

"You won't be able to take my fortune, you may be able to look like me but you won't know what I know." Tex stammered, one last plea of the dying.

The formless being didn't want any of that. All they wanted was justice and ownership of the mine in which their family died. One they got publicly, legally, and with plenty of witnesses. The other was a private thing.

"Other than your life I have taken everything that I have ever wanted from you." The creature finally broke their silence with vinegar on their tongue.

"My race can take any form it wants, be anything it wants," their voice rose to dangerous levels, again oozing through the faces of Tex's victims. "All I ever wanted was to be part of something. I found a family, and you took that away from me!"

"You're dying and no one is coming," they informed him. "Confess and I will end it quick," they teased,"or I can make this last all night."

"I could easily close off your airways or full your lungs with my being until it's almost too late." The slime wore the face of the charming man from the alley now. "No one will care that you're dead, I have left your empire to your abused underlings."

Tex's eyes bulged and widened one more time. The left one dislodged a bit from its socket.

"I have been meeting with your attorney," they said, now wearing Tex's own face and talking with his ridiculous accent. "It's over."

Every muscle in Tex's engulfed body finally released as he finally admitted defeat. His body seemed to accept it too, as they felt the warm premortem fluids begin to ooze from his pelvis.

"I was angry," Tex's voice was just a broken murmur. "The mine didn't produce the Arcanium I was promised." He tried to raise his voice in anger, but just coughed more droplets of blood. " I blamed them, so I just brought the whole mine down on top O' the pathetic lot. I figured I was doing them a favor."

"CRICKKKT!"

* * * * *

The slime waited several days after Tex's neck snapped,

hiding formless in the rafters, before they made their escape.

Within those same few days Corvaire had acquired most of

Tex's legal holdings (and likely all his illegal ones), as his

recently corrected will had dictated. All, of course, but the

largest brothel in the City on the Edge of Night, which now

belonged to a retired half-elf entertainer named Althea. No

one seemed to really care, as the ooze had hoped, and soon

they were on the back of an astral drake hopping asteroids

toward their new mine.

When the ooze reached what was the last resting place of the

only family they had ever known, they had hung their new

sign, "the Beggars Tomb," and found a good spot to play the

rubab to their adopted family that had finally been avenged.

Find more of my work:

https://www.2DMOld.com

https://www.Punteez.myshopify.com

2DMOld on Youtube

www.ingramcontent.com/pod-product-compliance
Lightning Source LLC
Chambersburg PA
CBHW070738160726
48003CB00006BA/2562